CU00872373

MAX AND KATIE'S

STUART ADVENTURE

BY SAMANTHA METCALF

ILLUSTRATED BY IAN R. WARD

Published in Great Britain in 2017 by:
Mysteries in Time Limited
www.mysteriesintime.com

Reprinted 2021

Illustrated by Ian R. Ward
www.ianrward.co.uk

A catalogue record for this book is available from the British Library.

ISBN 978-1-9997257-1-6

Hi! I'm Katie and I am 8 years old. I think my favourite thing is playing outside in any weather. I love going to the park, especially the adventure playground with the huge, curly slide. You can go really fast on that one, especially when you lie down!

Mum hates it when I come home covered in mud, but I can't help it. The fun parts of the park are always the muddiest.

Max is my older brother. He's really clever. He helps me with my homework when I'm stuck. He knows everything! But don't tell him I said that.

My brother always looks out for me. And we have lots of fun playing games together.

Hey, I'm Max and I'm 11. I love reading. I read comics and cartoons that make me laugh, and I read adventure stories about knights and castles, or pirates and buried treasure.

I also love solving puzzles. Grandpa always buys me books full of word-searches and crosswords. I like to time myself and see how fast I can solve them.

Katie is my younger sister. She is really energetic and fun to be around, even though she can't sit still for more than five minutes! She's really fast and sporty. I wish I could be as good as her at sports. But don't tell her I said that.

1

Max and Katie opened their eyes wide as the colours fizzed brightly in front of them. It was Bonfire Night and they were in their garden with Mum and Grandpa, excited about the fireworks.

Mum had given them each a sparkler and carefully lit it for them, before stepping back with a smile on her face.

Katie wasn't so sure about it. "The sparks are going to hurt my hand!" she squealed.

"They won't hurt you, not if you hold them away from your face and body," assured Max, who had been allowed to use sparklers before.

They were both mesmerised by the dancing sparks that flew out from the sizzling sparklers, then disappeared into the night air around them.

Katie shivered as a gust of wind whirled around them. She was grateful for the warmth from the bonfire that Grandpa had made.

Max was suddenly laughing.

Katie looked up sharply.

His laugh was infectious and she started to giggle with him. "What's so funny?"

"You go cross-eyed when you stare at the sparkler!" he exclaimed.

Katie smiled and shrugged. The sparks did merge together the more she stared, which made her vision blur and go fuzzy. She didn't care. She couldn't take her eyes off the bright sparkler.

As the sparkler fizzled out, Katie asked Grandpa to explain why they celebrate Bonfire Night.

"Well Katie, about four hundred years ago on 5th November 1605, when the Stuarts were on the throne, there was a plot to blow up the Houses of Parliament," he explained. "They didn't succeed, because they were caught before they could set fire to the gunpowder. But one man called Guy Fawkes was caught red-handed. He was arrested and sentenced to death."

Max was confused. "So we celebrate the fact that the Houses of Parliament DIDN'T get blown into tiny pieces, by setting off fireworks and lighting bonfires?"

Katie laughed. "That doesn't make any sense!"

Grandpa laughed at Max's confusion. "Yes, I

agree, it does sound strange!"

Grandpa turned and added another piece of wood to the bonfire. Max watched as sparks flew up into the air and the smoke billowed towards them.

"Just take a step back, young Max," suggested Grandpa. "Fire can spread very quickly and it can be very unpredictable. But smoke will also make you cough. Try to breathe some fresh air or cover your mouth with your scarf."

Max followed these suggestions.

It was time for Grandpa to light the fireworks.

Everyone stood back at a safe distance as Grandpa lit the rockets, which squealed as they flew into the air, then exploded into a burst of angry red light. These were Max's favourite fireworks.

"Ooh," they all said together. "Ahhhhh!"

Katie loved the ones that gently burst into purple sprinkles that gently fell down like raindrops.

After the firework display was finished,

Mum disappeared inside for a few minutes, then reappeared with mugs of hot chocolate. As the bonfire flames shrank and settled into a warm glow, she gave them marshmallows to toast. Max blew on his melted marshmallow before eating it, but Katie dropped hers into her hot chocolate and stirred it until it was even more gooey.

"Thanks, Guy Fawkes!" said Katie. "Bad luck for you, but I like this tradition!"

2

The next morning, Max heard the postman knocking on the door. He had a distinctive knock: rat-a-tat-tat.

Max jumped out of bed and raced down in his pyjamas to accept the turquoise box from his mum's outstretched arms.

He quickly turned and raced back upstairs with the new adventure. Katie was emerging from her room, yawning noisily and stretching her arms.

She followed Max sleepily into his room, where they opened the new box to find out where their next adventure would take them.

Max pulled out the Mission Plan and grinned.

"We're going back to the time of the Stuarts!" exclaimed Max.

"I hope we don't get caught up with the Gunpowder Plot," said Katie anxiously.

Mission Plan

Place: London
Date: AD 1666

In 1666, the Great Fire of London was raging
across the city. By the time the fire was put
out, most of the city was destroyed. Thousands
of people lost their homes.

Hidden in the home of John Taylor's family
home was a letter that proved a man's
innocence.

Task:

Find the hidden letter before the truth is
lost forever in the fire.

3

Max waited patiently. He knew his sister would be relieved that they weren't going to be caught up in the Gunpowder Plot. Instead, he knew that there was a much bigger threat: the Great Fire of London.

"FIRE???" shrieked Katie. "And not just any old fire. A fire that has the word 'great' in front of it. I'm sure that doesn't mean it was a fantastic fire either."

Max smiled. "No, the Great Fire of London got its name because of its massive size. But the good news is not many people died, so we should be safe."

"SHOULD be safe?!" Katie's cheeks were getting red with the worry. "The whole city burnt down!"

"Sshhh," hissed Max. "We don't want Mum to hear."

Katie took a few deep breaths to calm herself down. "OK, let's find out more about the time."

Max opened up the history magazine and started

reading. They learnt all about the Stuarts.

"Oh look!" exclaimed Katie. "There's Guy Fawkes. Grandpa was right!"

Max wondered how often his sister must doubt their Grandpa's knowledge.

They learnt about the English Civil War with the Roundheads and the Cavaliers; they read all about Oliver Cromwell and how the country changed while he was in power; they learnt about how the monarchy was brought back with the coronation of King Charles II. They soon reached the information about the Great Fire of London.

"At least it wiped out the terrible plague," said Max, trying to find all the positives from the tragedy. "And the city was rebuilt with St Paul's Cathedral as we know it today!"

Katie nodded quietly. "What will we wear?"

"We need to visit Grandpa's fancy dress shop," replied Max. "Come on, let's get dressed."

4

Max and Katie told Mum they were going to visit Grandpa to ask him some more about the Gunpowder Plot. Katie thought Mum would see through their plan; she would know this was a lie. But Max was right. Mum just smiled and told them to be careful.

Once they reached Grandpa's shop, they found the door was locked. They sheltered their eyes and peered through the window, steaming up the glass with their hot breath. They could see Grandpa, sitting at the payment counter, resting his chin on his upturned palm.

He was fast asleep!

Max and Katie giggled as they knocked on the door and Grandpa jumped so suddenly that he nearly fell off his stool!

When he spotted his grandchildren at the door,

he stretched sleepily with his arms out wide, then came and unlocked the door.

"I'm sorry," he yawned. "Last night was very late for me! Late nights are not easy to cope with at my age. Now, what can I do for you today?"

Max and Katie explained that they wanted to dress like someone from the Stuart era, after learning all about the Gunpowder Plot last night."

Grandpa looked thrilled. "Follow me," he smiled.

Katie was very excited, because she was able to choose a beautiful dress this time. It had thick sleeves and a full skirt the colour of gold, with a light pink body. She walked backwards and forwards, watching the way the skirt swished as she walked. She twirled on the spot and was delighted by the way the skirt filled with air like a parachute. She felt like a princess.

Max wasn't so happy. His clothes were fancy, with a frilly shirt and a hat with a large feather for

decoration.

But this wasn't the problem.

It was the wig he had to wear that made his face go pale.

Of course, Katie didn't help. She burst into uncontrollable giggles at the sight of her brother in a long wig.

Max scowled at his sister. "It was the fashion," he grumbled. "I would stand out like a sore thumb if I wore my hair short."

When Katie had finally got her laughter under control, Max and Katie thanked their Grandpa and headed home.

Max was very pleased that it was so early on a Saturday morning, because it meant the streets were unusually quiet. There were no neighbours out and about who might see them in their strange clothes.

5

Back home, they managed to sneak upstairs without Mum seeing them. Max called from the top of the stairs to tell her they were home.

They went straight into Max's bedroom, where they shut the door gently behind them.

Max handed Katie the Time Travel Sticker, which was the picture of a crown.

"In 1666, the Republic had already been overthrown and there was a king once again," explained Max. "It's important that we show we are

STUARTS

mysteries in time.
adventures through history

in support of the king."

"True," agreed Katie. "We don't want to get arrested for being supporters of Oliver Cromwell."

Max programmed the Time Machine to take them back to 1666. They got themselves in position and Katie pushed the large red button to start their journey through time.

Katie felt her long skirt swirl around her, while Max had to hang on to his wig and hat as they felt themselves spin through history.

They arrived on solid ground and Max straightened his wonky wig, before looking around.

They were on a narrow street with wooden houses on either side. Max suddenly became aware of the sound of crackling, just like the bonfire last night.

It was the sound of wood burning.

And it was very, very close.

6

The night sky was black with thick smoke, but the street was lit up with the light of the flames that were rising high above the buildings. The fire had been raging for four days already.

Max and Katie followed the sound of some people shouting frantically. They turned a corner and saw a man in a large hat holding a long metal rod.

"What's he doing with that?" asked Katie. "Even I know a bucket of water would work better against a fire than a metal rod. No wonder the city burnt down."

"That's called a fire hook," explained Max. "He's pulling down the houses with it, before the fire can get here and burn them."

"But that makes no sense!" exclaimed Katie. "The fire will damage the houses anyway, so why bother pulling them down first?"

"It's to make a fire break. If there are no houses in the path of the fire, then the fire can't spread."

Katie nodded. That made sense. If they could clear the wood that was fuelling the fire from its path, then they could stop the fire from spreading.

Max spotted a bucket nearby and ran to fill it up from the nearby well. Max and Katie tried their best to help by dousing the nearby flames with water, but the fire was too strong. There was a breeze that was fanning the flames, encouraging it to spread.

Suddenly, a voice yelled at them to watch out. Max spun round and watched with horror as the building was starting to crumble.

At that moment, a large beam of burning wood became dislodged by the flames and became detached from the building.

Max froze as he saw the enormous beam start to fall down towards where they were standing.

Katie threw her hands up to protect herself.

They both braced for impact.

7

Katie had expected the impact to come from above, so when she felt something hit her sideways, she was confused. She realised her eyes were tightly shut.

Someone must have pushed them to safety. Thankfully, she had landed on soft ground. As she opened her eyes and started to move, she heard Max cry out.

"Ouch!" he shrieked.

She realised that the soft ground she had landed on was actually her brother! She was lying across Max, but safely away from the burning beam.

"Sorry Max!" she said as she struggled to get up. Just then, a hand reached out to her from above.

"Here, take my hand," said the voice that belonged to the arm.

Katie did so and this mysterious stranger helped

her up.

"Thank you!" she said, brushing herself down.

Max was also now standing and straightening his clothes.

"Was it you who pushed us to safety?" asked Max.

The kind stranger dipped his head in a bow and waved his hand in front of him.

"I'm John Taylor, very pleased to meet you," he said.

Max introduced himself and Katie.

"Come on, let's get away from this burning building" said John. He then turned and led Max and Katie to a safer place away from the fire.

As they walked down to the river, Katie kept nudging Max in the side. Max understood. This was the person they were looking for, the person they had been sent here to help.

They stopped by the River Thames, which was still untouched by the fire, and breathed in the fresh air.

There were people everywhere loading their belongings into boats. People must have evacuated their homes and taken as much as they could carry to safety. There were people with boats charging double, even triple what it should cost to row them to the other side.

"That's daylight robbery!" exclaimed John. "People are making money when they should be coming together to help each other."

They had to dodge out of the path of another overloaded cart.

"Thank you for saving us," said Max. "You saved our lives."

John smiled. "No problem. We are losing the city at a frightening speed, but as far as we know, everyone has been pulled to safety."

"What can we do to help?" asked Max.

"I need to go back to my house and check my mother has escaped," replied John. "The wind has turned and I fear the house could be in its new path. If you'd like to come with me, I would appreciate your help to get her to safety if she is still there."

Max and Katie both nodded eagerly. This was their chance to look for the letter that would soon be lost forever.

"Of course!" replied Katie. "Let's go!"

8

Max and Katie followed John through the city's streets. They had to dodge people pushing their worldly possessions in large carts or balancing too many things in their arms. There were people crying as they watched their home disappear in flames.

They arrived at a house just as its door was pulled open by a man holding a fire hook.

"Uncle Geoffrey!" exclaimed John. "I came to check that Mum is safe."

John's uncle smiled. "She is safe. Our neighbour led her to safety an hour ago."

"Great news. I see you are going to help stop the fire," said John, looking at the large fire hook in his uncle's hand. "I'll come with you."

"Would you like us to check your house for you?" asked Max. "We can carry some of your belongings to safety."

John smiled. "That's very kind of you. But be quick, and only take what you can carry easily. Make sure you don't get trapped inside in case the wind changes. No belongings are worth getting hurt over."

Max and Katie nodded. They agreed a place to meet, then waved John and Geoffrey off.

Max and Katie then entered the house to search for the important letter. The rooms were dark, because the windows were small and covered with wooden shutters. The furniture was simple, but looked heavy and hand-made. It was a shame that this would probably all be burnt to ashes soon.

"We need to move fast," urged Katie. "I know we don't want to fail the mission by not finding the letter, but it's more of a fail if we don't make it out safely."

They started their search. They opened drawers and cupboards, pulled books off the shelves. They were looking for loose sheets hidden between the pages. They even looked behind paintings and underneath rugs.

"This is hopeless!" cried Max. "We don't even know what the letter is about, so how will we recognise it if we see it?!"

Just as they were despairing, Katie spotted something strange.

"What's that?" she asked, seeing some strange marks carved into one of the wooden floorboards below the window.

Max came closer, opening the window shutters fully to cast some light from outside. Katie realised that the light was coming from the uncontrollable flames that were now raging higher than the buildings in the city.

They both leaned closer to the marks and realised it was a date: 1649.

"1649," read Max. "The year that King Charles I

was executed."

Max looked closer and realised that the floorboard with the date carved into it was loose. "Here, help me lift this up," he said to Katie.

Together, they eased the floorboard up and found a piece of paper hidden beneath.

"Bingo!" exclaimed Max.

They were so busy trying to read what the letter said, that they didn't notice the shadow creep up on them, nor did they hear the footsteps crossing the floor towards them.

Suddenly, they were both pushed forward and the letter flew into the air.

Katie had lost her balance and she fell on her side, while Max's wig fell down over his eyes. They heard heavy footsteps running back down the stairs and out through the door. But before they could look out of the window, there was an enormous explosion that sounded very close.

"The letter!" said Max. They looked around, but it was gone. They both knew the person who had pushed them must have stolen it.

The letter was gone and they had no idea what secrets it held.

What was this person trying to hide?

9

There was no time to think about it now.

"What was that explosion?" asked Katie anxiously.

"It was either the fire reaching the barrels of gunpowder down at the docks, or the order has been given to start blowing up houses to make a larger fire break," explained Max.

"But they were pulling houses down with fire hooks!" shrieked Katie.

"I read about this earlier. The people fighting the fires got desperate. Because the wind fanned the fire even more, the fire was able to jump over large fire breaks. They couldn't pull down houses quickly enough before the fire spread past the fire break," replied Max.

"But wouldn't explosions cause more fire?" asked Katie.

"It was worth the risk to try to stop the fire. It was definitely going to spread if they didn't use gunpowder, so they may as well try using it. It was worth a chance."

"Then we need to move," urged Katie, imagining getting caught up in an explosion. "And fast."

10

Max agreed. They gathered a few small items as they left, then raced down the stairs and outside into the chaos of people running for their lives.

They started racing back the way they had come, when they heard a voice calling for help.

"Where is that voice coming from?" asked Katie.

They listened carefully and realised it was coming from around the corner. They quickly went to investigate and saw John's uncle lying on the ground, his legs trapped by a large wooden beam.

"Thank goodness!" cried Geoffrey, coughing from the smoke. "I thought nobody could hear me!"

"Hold still," said Max. "Katie, help me pull this off. As soon as you can move, try to pull your legs out."

Max and Katie pulled with all their strength to lift the beam. They were struggling. It was too heavy!

Suddenly, they heard a whoosh!

They looked up and realised the flames had reached John's home and were leaping across to the nearest building.

They had escaped just in time.

"Leave me," yelled John's uncle "Save yourselves."

Max and Katie looked at each other. They knew they were thinking the same thing. They weren't

going to leave him here. They had to help him.

They nodded at each other then pulled using all their strength.

They couldn't believe their luck when the beam lifted slightly, enough to allow John's uncle to move his legs a little.

"Nearly!" shouted Geoffrey. "Nearly there!"

Katie could feel her grip loosen. She couldn't hold on for much longer. They gave one final heave.

Just as she felt her fingertips start to slip, Geoffrey pulled his legs fully out.

He was free!

As they helped Geoffrey up, they noticed a piece of paper slip from his pocket. The piece of paper had familiar writing. It was the stolen letter!

They all looked at the letter, then looked at each other.

There was no time to talk now.

They had to escape.

11

Max and Katie helped Geoffrey down to the river's edge. His leg was hurt and he was limping uncomfortably.

They found a place to rest by the river and sat down to catch their breath.

Just then, they heard a familiar voice.

"What happened?" asked John, as he rushed closer.

"We're all OK," said Geoffrey. "Max and Katie here saved my life."

They explained what had happened, then there was an awkward silence as Max and Katie were looking at the letter that Geoffrey was clutching in his right hand.

Geoffrey looked from Max and Katie to the letter. He took a deep breath and held the letter out to John, who looked confused.

"Wh- what's this?" he asked. "Why do you look so serious?"

"It's a letter that was sent to your father, before he was arrested," replied his uncle.

"Why are you showing this to me now?" John's voice was starting to sound nervous. "Why have you kept it all this time?"

"Just read it and see."

John took the letter and looked at it with a frown, before waving it away angrily.

"I can't read," he said.

Max reached out his hand. "Would you like me to read it for you?"

John looked at Max with a serious expression, before reluctantly handing it over.

"Thank you Max," he said quietly.

Max smoothed out the letter and started reading.

1649

For the attention of Master Geoffrey Taylor,

This is a warrant for your arrest. You are accused of being a traitor of the Republic, for your support of the king and crown. If found guilty, you will be executed.

Long live the Republic.

Oliver Cromwell

Oliver Cromwell

Lord Protector

12

Max finished reading and folded the letter quietly. Everyone was stunned into silence.

John was the first to speak. "This letter is addressed to you, Uncle. You were the one who was being arrested that day, not my father. All this time, all these years, I've been thinking my dad was taken

by Cromwell's men, that he was loyal to the king, when the truth is quite different!"

John's uncle was silent, with his head hanging down. He eventually raised his eyes and met the gaze of his nephew.

"I'm sorry, John," he said sadly. "It's time the truth came out. You father was a supporter of Oliver Cromwell. He had joined the Roundheads to fight against the king. It was me who was the supporter of

the king. I wanted the crown to stay as it was."

Max was amazed. Families must have been torn apart by the Civil War.

Katie was confused. "If John's father supported Oliver Cromwell, why was he arrested? Oliver Cromwell had won! He was in charge."

John's uncle rubbed his eyes. "The letter has my name on it, the soldiers were looking for me," he replied. "They had come to arrest me, but my brother lied to them and pretended to be me. So they took him instead."

"Why didn't you say something at the time?" asked John. "Why didn't you stop them?"

"I wasn't there. I was out with my friends plotting our next attack against Cromwell. By the time I got home, it was too late. He was gone. This letter was left behind."

"Did you ever see him again?" asked Katie gently.

John's uncle nodded. "I went to the prison to

speak with him before he was executed. I demanded to know why he had done this. He said he had to protect me, he had to protect his little brother. I told him I would tell the guards the truth, but he stopped me. He said they would arrest us both. He was right. They wouldn't have believed me. He saved my life."

John sniffed noisily. "Did he say anything about me?"

"Of course," replied Geoffrey. "He told me to look after you and bring you up like my own son. You were too young to understand, just a baby. Then, when Oliver Cromwell was overthrown and the crown was restored, I decided to keep the lie going. I wanted you to only think favourably of your father. I realised you could always think of him as a supporter of the king. You could think of him as a tragic hero, not a traitor. I am sorry I lied, but I thought I was helping you at the time."

"Don't worry Uncle," sniffed John. "I am still

proud of my dad. I don't care what his beliefs were, at least he was fighting for what he believed in."

13

Just then, they heard some frantic shouting just behind them. They all turned in the direction of the noise, where they were amazed to see an enormous ship that was decorated with gold. Katie gasped at how grand it looked.

The fire had reached the houses on the water's edge and there was a line of people passing buckets of water from the river. Max and Katie joined the line of people like a human chain and helped pass buckets full of water from the river along the line to be thrown at the fire, then passed the empty buckets back down towards the river to be refilled.

John had stopped in his tracks. He was staring at a man throwing a bucket of water over the nearby fire. John was mesmerised.

Max and Katie went to find out what was wrong. "Is everything OK, John?" asked Max. "Do you

know him?"

John looked shocked at Max.

"You don't recognise him?!" he asked.

Max looked again, but shook his head.

"But that's the King!" he exclaimed. "That's King
Charles II!"

Max and Katie looked back at this man and
realised he was dressed in very fancy clothes, but
they were now dirty and he had rolled his sleeves up

to his elbows.

Katie was suddenly star-struck.

"I've never met royalty before," she said, trying to straighten her hair and brush off some dirt from her dress. She practised doing a curtsey, bowing her head low as she did so.

"Er, I think he's a bit busy at the moment," said Max, pulling her away by the arm. "Come on, we need to help fight this last part of the fire!"

Katie scowled at Max and shook his hand away. She knew he was right.

She took one last look at King Charles II, then rejoined the fight against the fire.

14

The fire was now under control. Max and Katie thought it was time to leave John and his uncle in peace.

Max and Katie said their goodbyes and walked along the river towards the sunrise. They walked past two gentlemen, who were looking out over the city, watching the final smoke rise from the distant St Paul's Cathedral.

One man with a thick, curly wig was clutching a book that said 'Diary' on the side.

"I hope the cheese that I buried will survive the fire!" sighed the man clutching the diary. "So, Christopher, what do you think? What will happen to our city?"

"Well, Samuel," replied the other man. "I have a vision of a grand city made from brick and stone, a strong city, one that will be admired from afar for

hundreds of years to come."

It was Max's turn to stop in his tracks.

Katie hadn't realised for several steps. She had even started talking to him, before she realised she was talking to thin air.

Katie turned around and realised he was listening to the conversation between these two gentlemen.

"What is it, Max?" she asked. "What have you

heard?"

"Do you know who these two are?" he asked excitedly.

Katie looked at them and shook her head. "If I didn't even recognise the king earlier, how would I know who these two are?!"

Max could barely contain his excitement.

"The man on the left is Samuel Pepys, who wrote a very famous diary that we learnt about in school," he started. "And the other man is Sir Christopher Wren, the famous architect. He designed St Paul's Cathedral, as well as the Monument to commemorate the Great Fire of London!"

Katie shrugged. "The king was way more impressive than a writer and an architect."

15

The fire close to the river had now been put out. Everyone was resting on the river bank, exhausted.

The sun was starting to rise and the blue sky was visible, now that the blanket of smoke was clearing.

London lay in ruins, but there was hope now.

Max and Katie knew the facts: over 13,000 houses were burnt to the ground. But they also knew that there were surprisingly few people hurt. They knew that the city would be rebuilt even better than before, with impressive new buildings, such as St Paul's Cathedral. The houses would now be built from brick, not wood, in case of any future fire. They would also be built on wider streets that would eventually make way for cars and buses in about four hundred years' time.

Max and Katie felt a breeze swirl around their feet, rising up until they were fully wrapped in a colourful cloud of Time Travel.

They landed back in Max's bedroom, where they sat on the bed, exhausted. This adventure had been very dangerous.

"I don't ever want to fight another fire again," said Max. "Grandpa was right. Fire is so dangerous. It can spread so quickly and unpredictably."

Katie agreed. "But at least we got to meet a king."

"Er, we didn't actually meet him," corrected Max.

"That's not how I'm going to remember the story!" replied Katie happily.

Also in the Mysteries in Time series:

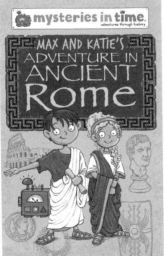

mysteries in time.
adventures through history

MAX AND KATIE'S
VIKING
ADVENTURE

mysteries in time.
adventures through history

MAX AND KATIE'S
ADVENTURE
IN ANCIENT
CHINA

mysteries in time.
adventures through history

MAX AND KATIE'S
SPACE
ADVENTURE

mysteries in time.
adventures through history

MAX AND KATIE'S
STUART
ADVENTURE